David's Grannies

MARY MILLS

David's Grannies by Mary Mills

ISBN 978-1-952027-44-4 (Paperback)
ISBN 978-1-952027-45-1 (Hardback)
ISBN 978-1-952027-46-8 (eBook)

New Leaf Media, LLC
175 S. 3rd Street, Suite 200
Columbus, OH 43215
www.thenewleafmedia.com

David had two grannies.

One was black and one was white.

David was a light brown colour.

He had black hair.

David's mummy's mummy was white – well, more pink than white.

He called her Nanna B because her name was Heather Bradley.

Bradley began with a "B".

David's daddy's mummy was black – well, more brown than black.

He called her Nanna P because her name was Gloria Perkins. Perkins began with a "P".

Sometimes he got them muddled up, as "B" and "P" sound nearly the same.

David loved both his grannies.

Nanna B was quite young.

She didn't look much like a granny at all.

She wore jeans and trainers and bright colourful jackets and she hadn't got any grey hair.

When Nanna B took David to the park, she would go down the slide with him, when no-one was looking!

When she took him to the swimming pool, she would climb
with him to the top of the elephant slide. They would both
slide down the trunk together – WHOOOOSH!
It was great fun!

Nanna B did not have a husband any more.

She lived in a flat with her cat called Mickey and dog called Honey.

When he went to Nanna B's home, he and Nanna B and Mickey would all sit together on the sofa. Honey would sleep on the floor nearby.

They would watch TV, eat chocolate biscuits and doughnuts and drink Coke.
It felt all warm and cosy.

David loved Nanna B. They had such a lot of fun together.

Nanna P lived in a different town, a long way away.

Sometimes David and his mum and dad went to visit Nanna P.

Her home was full of colourful things from Jamaica.

Nanna P cooked lovely things for them to eat – salt-fish, chicken, yams and ackee, and peas and rice.

Her house was always full of people.

David had lots of cousins to play with when he went there.

Nanna P was quite young, too.

She still had children at home to look after.

It was a very noisy home but there was lots of laughter.

MILK
FIVE STAR
UNITED

Sometimes Nanna P would come to David's house.

She always brought a big basket of food with her.

David's dad loved Nanna P's cooking!

David loved to sit with her and listen to her stories.

She promised to take him on holiday to Jamaica one day.

Jamaica
FiveStar UNITED
JAMAICA

David's grannies were very different.

He felt very lucky to have them!

He loved them both very much.

And they both loved him.

Activities

1. Do you have a granny?

2. What do you call your granny?

3. Can you draw a picture of her?

4. What do you like doing most with your granny?

Activities

1. Do you have a cat or dog?

2. What do you call them?

3. Do you like to play with them?

4. Can you draw a picture of a cat and dog?

Mary Mills – a mum and grandmother. Primary school teacher who has taught many children from different ethnic and cultural backgrounds. Wanted to write a book that could be read with a class of children or individuals and discussed and which would also be easy for children to read by themselves. Hoping to promote understanding of other lives.

1992 "Mission to find a missionary." YOURS mag. Autumn edition.

1993. "Pages from my Diary". YOURS mag, Summer Special.

1993 "A tour of Barrow-on-Trent." Derbyshire Now mag. October edition.

1993. "Pause for Thought at Christmas." Derbyshire Now mag. Dec. edition.

1998 "Back to your roots." Article for Church Article published News Service, April edition.

1998 "How wicked is wicked?" Article for Church News Service, July edition.

1998 Article published in New Christian Herald, Dec.16th edition, "Christmas under the mango trees." (About Uganda.)

1999 Revisions done for Scripture Union of "Tanglewoods' Secret" and "Treasures of the Snow." – children's Christian classics by Patricia St John.

1999 Letter of the Week in Woman's Weekly, July 13th edition.

1999 Article on Hospital Chaplaincy visiting in October edition of "Yours" magazine – "Patients Rewarded."

1999 Church of England Newspaper, Dec. 10th edition. Article on the revision of Patricia St John's children's classics.

2000 "Taking the paper to pieces." Article in Christian Herald. Jan. 29th edition, about the Christian Herald.

2000 Article in Times Educational Supplement on the Threshold payment for. teachers. Aug. 11th edition.

2000 Article in "Yours" mag – "A Christmas card comes to life." (A holiday in Switzerland.) December edition.

2001 "The Universe" (R.C. paper). Interview with George Alagiah. Feb. 4th edition.

2001 "Yours – Summer Special" mag – short article and photo of my granddaughter.

2001 "Village Voice" – local newspaper. Article "Out of Africa – but going back again!"

2001 Baptist Times, Oct. 11th edition. "Patricia St John for today's children."

2002 "Classics for a new generation." Article about Patricia St John books in C.N.S.

2002 Baptist Times. Article on trip to Ethiopia. "We *can* make a difference if we want to!" Feb. 21st edition.

2002 Letter of the Week in "Best" mag. – June 11th edition.

2002 Letter in "Take a Break" mag. About Ugandan pastor's visit to U.K. Aug. 15th edition.

2002 Baptist Times – "It's the real chicken run!" – article about a Christian farmer who runs a scheme to help Young Offenders on his chicken farm in Derbyshire. Sept. 5th edition.

2002 Baptist Times – Article on the recent earthquake in the Midlands. (came out in Oct. 3rd edition.)

2016 YOURS mag (Jan. edition) "Love changes everything" – Article about moving to Africa.

2016 Dogs Monthly. (March edition.) "A different view". – Article about bringing my dog and cat back from Uganda to UK.

2018-2019 –   Three "Letter of the Week" letters in Your View, Daily Mail Week-end Magazine.

2018 Chapter in ACW Christmas Anthology. "Christmas WITH Bethlehem."

2020 "Look at me now!" Article about bringing a dog over from Uganda in "animalwatch" mag – for Anglican Soc. for Welfare of Animals.

**Writing Biography – Mary Mills. (Former Non-Commercial Writers'
Co-ordinator for the Association of Christian Writers.)**

I started writing as a child and have always enjoyed putting pen to paper
– far preferring this means of communication to performing in public "up
front." I have always been a prolific letter-writer.

A teacher by profession, but becoming increasingly disillusioned with the
Education system, I undertook a Correspondence Course with the Writer's
Bureau in 1990, hoping it might lead to a new career! This started me
seriously writing, and having to send off articles for hopeful publication
focussed my attention on an enjoyable means of communication which
really suited me.

I have since written, and had published, many articles on various topics,
writing for Christian and secular publications. I am a frequent visitor to
Africa (Uganda and Ethiopia in particular) and this is a constant source of
material for articles which hopefully help to raise awareness and bring a
response in the form of securing sponsorships for those I meet.

I have also revised six of Patricia St John's Classic Children's stories for
Scripture Union, making the language more friendly for Millennium-aged
readers. These include:

"Treasures of the Snow."
"Tanglewoods' Secret."
"Rainbow Garden"
"The Mystery of Pheasant Cottage"
"Star of Light."
"The Secret of the Fourth Candle."

I have helped to have two of these translated into Amharic, for Ethiopian readers, and a third – "Star of Light" is currently being translated and subsequently published.

Through being a member of ACW, and serving on the Committee for six years, I have been able to reach many folk and hopefully help them in their own writing endeavours through networking contacts formed through the Association.

I had the privilege of interviewing George Alagiah in 2003 and the article was published in "Yours" magazine and "The Universe" (Roman Catholic newspaper.)

Mary Mills.

www.ingramcontent.com/pod-product-compliance
Lightning Source LLC
Chambersburg PA
CBHW041923180726
48295CB00002B/59